Eloise Decorates for Christmas

KAY THOMPSON'S ELOISE
Eloise Decorates for Christmas

STORY BY **Lisa McClatchy**

ILLUSTRATED BY **Tammie Lyon**

Ready-to-Read

Simon Spotlight

New York   London   Toronto   Sydney   New Delhi

SIMON SPOTLIGHT
An imprint of Simon & Schuster Children's Publishing Division
1230 Avenue of the Americas, New York, NY 10020
First Simon Spotlight hardcover edition September 2016
First Aladdin Paperbacks edition October 2007
Copyright © 2007 by the Estate of Kay Thompson
All rights reserved, including the right of reproduction in whole or in part in any form.
"Eloise" and related marks are trademarks of the Estate of Kay Thompson.
SIMON SPOTLIGHT, READY-TO-READ, and colophon are registered
trademarks of Simon & Schuster, Inc.
For information about special discounts for bulk purchases, please contact Simon & Schuster
Special Sales at 1-866-506-1949 or business@simonandschuster.com.
The text of this book was set in Century Old Style.
Manufactured in the United States of America 0816 LAK
2 4 6 8 10 9 7 5 3 1
Library of Congress Control Number 2006940006
ISBN 978-1-4814-6747-6 (hc)
ISBN 978-1-4169-4978-7 (pbk)

I am Eloise.
I am six.

I live at The Plaza Hotel.
The hotel is busy today.
Deliverers are delivering.
Decorators are decorating.

"What is going on?" I say.
"They are getting ready
    for Christmas," Nanny says.

"I am going to help," I say.

"Eloise, you are to stay here," Nanny says. "We have our own tree to decorate."

Yes, we do.
But the tree downstairs
will be much more fun.

Skipperdee, Weenie, and I
sneak out the door.

We deck the halls
with Christmas cheer.

We jingle down to the lobby.
I pick flowers for Nanny
on the way.

Look, a pretty red
ribbon for my hair.

And garland for Skipperdee.

And silver bells for Weenie.

We arrive in the lobby.
"Merry Christmas, Eloise!"
the manager says.
"Do you like the tree?"

Oh yes, I do.
But something is missing.

It needs a star.

The silver bow on this present is just right.

"Where are you going,
Eloise?" the manager says.

"To fix the tree," I say.

Weenie and I sail up
to the tippy-tippy top
of the tree.

"Oh dear. Oh dear.
Come down here at once,
Eloise," Nanny says.

I slide, slide, slide down.

I jump into Nanny's arms.

"Merry Christmas,
Nanny," I say.
Oh, I love, love, love
Christmas!